Put Beginning Readers on the Right Track with
ALL ABOARD READING™

The All Aboard Reading series is especially designed for beginning readers. Written by noted authors and illustrated in full color, these are books that children really want to read—books to excite their imagination, expand their interests, make them laugh, and support their feelings. With fiction and nonfiction stories that are high interest and curriculum-related, All Aboard Reading books offer something for every young reader. And with four different reading levels, the All Aboard Reading series lets you choose which books are most appropriate for your children and their growing abilities.

Picture Readers
Picture Readers have super-simple texts, with many nouns appearing as rebus pictures. At the end of each book are 24 flash cards—on one side is a rebus picture; on the other side is the written-out word.

Station Stop 1
Station Stop 1 books are best for children who have just begun to read. Simple words and big type make these early reading experiences more comfortable. Picture clues help children to figure out the words on the page. Lots of repetition throughout the text helps children to predict the next word or phrase—an essential step in developing word recognition.

Station Stop 2
Station Stop 2 books are written specifically for children who are reading with help. Short sentences make it easier for early readers to understand what they are reading. Simple plots and simple dialogue help children with reading comprehension.

Station Stop 3
Station Stop 3 books are perfect for children who are reading alone. With longer text and harder words, these books appeal to children who have mastered basic reading skills. More complex stories captivate children who are ready for more challenging books.

In addition to All Aboard Reading books, look for All Aboard Math Readers™ (fiction stories that teach math concepts children are learning in school) and All Aboard Science Readers™ (nonfiction books that explore the most fascinating science topics in age-appropriate language).

All Aboard for happy reading!

For Amanda, Jessica, and Katie, who live
across the street—J.H.

To Kumari—D.P.

Library of Congress Cataloging-in-Publication Data is available.

ISBN 0-448-42674-9   E F G H I J

The Gingerbread Kid
Goes to School

By Joan Holub
Illustrated by Debbie Palen

Grosset & Dunlap • New York

One day, the principal
baked a gingerbread kid.
He took it
in his lunch box.

Oh, no!
Something was missing!
The principal put on
two candy eyes.

Suddenly,
the gingerbread
kid winked.

He did a flip
off the desk.

He did a cartwheel
on the floor.
Then he ran away.

"Come back!" shouted
the principal.

The principal ran after
the gingerbread kid.

The gingerbread kid laughed
and shouted,
"I'm the gingerbread kid.
I'm fast as can be.
You can run, run, run.
But you can't catch me!"

The gingerbread kid ran
to the playground.

He kicked a ball
over the fence.

"Come back!"
shouted two gym coaches.
Then they ran after him.

The gingerbread kid laughed
and shouted,
"I'm the gingerbread kid.
I'm fast as can be.
You can run, run, run.
But you can't catch me!"

The gingerbread kid ran
into the lunchroom.

He hopped in
the beans
and the rice.

"Come back!"
shouted the three lunch ladies.
They dropped their spoons
and ran after him.

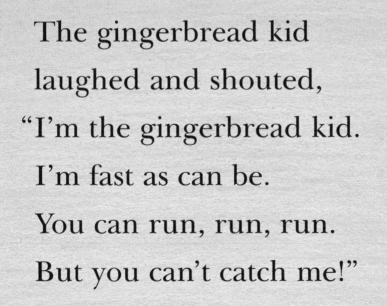

The gingerbread kid

laughed and shouted,

"I'm the gingerbread kid.

I'm fast as can be.

You can run, run, run.

But you can't catch me!"

The gingerbread kid ran by
four teachers in the hall.
He spilled their jars of paint.

"Come back!" they shouted.
Then they ran after him.

LIBRARY

The gingerbread kid
laughed and shouted,
"I'm the gingerbread kid.
I'm fast as can be.
You can run, run, run.
But you can't catch me!"

The gingerbread kid ran
into the library.

He jumped on a boy's desk.

"Chase me,"

said the gingerbread kid.

The boy kept reading.

"CHASE ME!"

shouted the gingerbread kid.

The boy shook his head.

"What kind of kid wants to read?"

asked the gingerbread kid.

"A smart kid,"

said the boy.

"Not as smart as me,"
said the gingerbread kid.
"I ran away from the principal,
two gym coaches,
three lunch ladies,
and four teachers.
I can run away from you, too!"

"No. You can't," said the boy.
"Here are five reasons why."
The boy made a fist.

One by one,
he held up his fingers.
"One.
Two.
Three.
Four.
FIVE."

Then he grabbed
the gingerbread kid.
"Gotcha!" the boy said.

Like magic,
the gingerbread kid
turned into a cookie again.

Suddenly,

everyone ran into the library.

The four teachers bumped
into the three lunch ladies.
The three lunch ladies bumped
into the two gym coaches.
The two gym coaches bumped
into the principal.
And the principal bumped
into the boy.
Oops!
The gingerbread kid cookie
went right out the window.

And right outside,
the smart boy's smart dog
was waiting.
Chomp! Chomp!